Printed in the United States of America
ISBN: 978-1548689339
First Printing: July 2017
NealJessicaWriter@gmail.com

SHORT ADVENTURES OF A LOOOONG DOG

Jessica Neal

It was a bright day for a walk in the sunny park,
A sunshine day for a dog with a funny bark.
"Tjirp, Tjirp!" heard the dog from a tree,
In a nest sang not one bird, but three!

Down the pathway rode his best friend on a bike,
His name was not Spot or Fluffy, but Mike.
Mike greeted him friendly and the dog wagged his tail,
Riding off to deliver the neighborhood's mail.

The dog had to go, he smelled something sweet,
Off to the ice cream man, who always gave him a treat
Something that tastes better than a meaty bone,
Free scoops of ice cream on a vanilla cone.

"I don't believe we've met before."
Said the dog and held out his paw.
"Quack-Quack!" yelled one. "Quack-Quack!" cried another,
"That's the dog who barked at my brother!"

He saw something bouncing and round and red,
Some boys were kicking it with their feet and their head.
"Woof-Woof!" he barked while chasing the ball,
He tried to bite it, but his mouth was too small.

He heard four loud dog voices coming from afar,
A Bulldog, two pugs and one with a scar.
They started talking about the fastest car around,
Their owners, babies and the prettiest lady hound.

Something came flying out of the sky,
There it goes again soaring so high!
"I've got to have it and grab it! What could it be!"
Said the owner: 'Hey, dog, give us back our frisbee!"

After all the excitement, he felt his tummy rumble,
He wanted meaty dishes or an apple crumble.
"Hot dogs! Hot dogs!" he heard someone yell,
From a food cart came an amazing smell.

He couldn't wait to try the yelling man's food.
A sausage in a bun, it tastes so good!
"I don't know why they call it a dog that's hot,
It tastes much better than tacos, I kid you not!"

A drop of rain fell on the dog's nose,
On his ears, his back and his hairy toes.
When he looked up he saw with his doggy eyes
Cats and dogs raining from the skies.

On that rainy day he made many mates;
A green frog he met at the park's steel gates,
A white dove named Pearl and a snail called Andy,
He really liked meeting a lady Dachshund named Mandy.

Soaking wet he had a moment to ponder,
About this perfect day for a dog to wander.
He stood on all fours and started to wiggle,
To dry his fur coat. Then he heard a giggle.

In front of him sat a giggling rival,
What a way to make a sneaky arrival!
"Sorry, Cat, I cannot stay and talk!
Lovely to see you, but I've got to walk."

All came to a standstill when the dog did see,
The most alluring colors of pink, yellow and green.
On his nose sat a butterfly, so stunning and bright,
She flew away gracefully with the wind, like a kite.

After a very long day of running in the park,
The sun was setting, it was getting dark.
It was time to leave and go home to rest,
He wanted to see his owner, she is the best!

"What a good day!" the dog happily said,
His owner gave him a pat on the head.
Curling up, he settled in for the night,
Smiling and thinking: "This feels so right!"

Thank you for purchasing this book!
I invested a piece of my soul in the writing of this book.
I sincerely hope you and your kids were pleased with the story and enjoyed the time spent together in reading this book.
If you enjoyed the story, even a little, I would be grateful if you took a few minutes and wrote an honest review on Amazon.

I also love hearing from my readers!
Email me at NealJessicaWriter@gmail.com and say hello!
In the meantime, I will keep writing more stories to share with you and your kids.
Thank you for your time, and happy reading!

With love,
Jessica Neal

Loooong Dog's Adventures Book Series

More Books by Jessica Neal

Made in the USA
Monee, IL
19 December 2019